DIAMOND

♥

COUNTRY GIRL

Automatiserad Teknik vilket används för att

Analysera text- och data i digital form i syfte att

Generalisera information, enligt 15a, 15b och 15c §§

Upphovsrättslagen (text- och data utvinning), är förbjuden

© Country Girl 2025

Publisher: BoD · Books on Demand, Östermalmstorg 1,

114 42 Stockholm, Sweden, bod@bod.se

Print: Libri Plureos GmbH, Friedensallee 273,

22763 Hamburg, Tyskland

ISBN: 978-91-8097-108-9

"I see the stars in your eyes"

you said, it was me that

put them there"

DIAMOND

♥

COUNTRY GIRL

Part One

I t was in my better days (it's my memories of the later 19th century)

I walked along my way. road was empty no one dare to be outside the weather was different then yesterday's rain. but it was changeable weather so, only one was me walking this road. The luck of my heart was this beautiful white horse I had so I always could ride to my beautiful girl of my heart.

I take a ride away with all my love in my chest to get to my precious sweet heart.

That's why I say the better happier days of the 19th century, it was love back then timeless love between a woman and a man but so young at heart I didn't always know to take care of her. My mouth sometimes said things I did not know she listen so well to my words so young at heart I wounded her heart oh! What a fool I was some of these days.

Always when I reached her big old house, I looked at the window at the right side of the house just to see if she was home, she used to have a little light for me her message I was welcome into her house. I used to park the horse a bit away from the house so her father not should see me or hear the horse. The horse was quiet and I was so happy for that. I picked up one little stone I always did this way so, if she was in her room, she knows it was me when she heard the noise of me.

So, beautiful she always was her loving voice when she talked to me. Welcomed me into her romantic room. I climbed up in this garden tree it was my only way to get inside, her father would not never let me in especial night-time like this. So, as I tell you I climbed up in the tree always so happy that it grows up there, I was like a gorgeous bird that used the tree she was always so light scared I would fall down or the tree would break. But I was a good climber like a bird I reach her window and she helped me inside again as so many times before, our secret love in this 19th century.

When I stood there in her room it always takes my breath away to see her. She was always worried of me if her father finds out I'm there he would get his big hands on me and I do not dare to know what he would do to me so, we always talking low even whispering about our love.

It was always my pleasure to see her so, romantic to kiss her cheek, her nose, and tell her my words only she knows, she knows me as the young hearted man I was these days I didn't know I hurted her when I left her because I foolish told her I would never ever take the big step to marriage. I was so young at heart I said I wanted to be free like a bird to her, so I hurted her. Her love was so sweet. When time to go home I reach my old horse, I was a happy young man of this 19th century. With a loving girl in his mind. So, I started the ride and left this house of love the horse I ride was always so nice and quietly. To take a ride especial to places of young hearted girls like mine. That's why I love this horse otherwise I had never got a chance to reach my sweet hearted girl of mine. What a night, when I reach my house I whistling along happy as I were with my thoughts of her, when I reach my house and the door, I notice the key was gone it was not in my pocket as it always use to be. I must have dropped it so; get into my house I just couldn't do.

Oh! what a bad luck I lose my key so probably it was in the romantic room with her so I went back to the street I loved saw the light was not on so I carefully throw a little stone on the window, no answer no light maybe she gets to sleep. I try to throw another stone, and one more stone then at last the light was on but it wasn't her it was the man with the big hands father of her he takes a look outside. He opens the window with a angry face and yell to me to go to another place I could hear from the background a worried voice begging please. He was so angry it would be dangerous if he had a grip on me. I was worried of her so scared she must be will he hurt her when I leave punish her. I try to talk explain I only a friend but he yells he's no fool and that I should leave and never return to this house and he told me if I do, he would shoot me down and put a bullet into my brain. So, I went away scared of his treat. I will try to connect with her again but it wouldn't be easy I understand.

Time went on I tried to not cause her any problems with her father so I walked quietly one night down her window the lamp was on the moon was full and there in the night it was a young man that missing his girl of heart. Wanted to tell her he missed her a lot but I was scared of the father of this house would shoot me down if he understood I stood there again. So is the life in the 19th century.

Some days later when I went back, last time I was at her house twice she didn't have any light for me maybe she slept so here I am stood here again wondering how to reach her again I wanted to tell her I wanted to hold her one more time. But who was I now ? what had her father said to her, so I stood there thinking in the dark night under her window what should I do. Wondering if I should dare to make some noise throw a little stone on her window to catch her intention. I did not want to cause her any more problems to her. Her father was a problem. I pick up a little stone held it in my right hand a little while, while I thinking about it must talk to her see if she is fine my little heart of mine, at last, I'm carefully as I could I throw the little stone that hopefully wake the connection between me and her. Maybe she didn't want to see me I must get some answers. Does she still love me?

So, I throw the stone the sound of it on the glass make my noise. Will she hear and let me in.

Nothing happened I wait pick another stone throw it on the glass I saw her now her face, her lovely soft hair reflection of her behind the glass, she quietly opens the window she looked scared and warned me if her father knows you here, he will become a monster hurt you bad please leave before it's too late but me a young hearted man said I only leave if you know I love you sweetheart.

She said to me all her love is for me but that I can't stay it to dangerous my father is cold man when you come around. He says I'm too young for that kind of love. He warned me to send me away if he sees you around this old house again.

I said that I will be back and throw her an air kiss she smiled and catch the kiss with her pale white sweet hand. And then she sent an air kiss back and said she loved me.

I catch her kiss smiled and said I try to find out a way for us to be together for some talking time. I pick up one flower in the green grass climb fast up in the tree like a bird I fly when I reach her I put the flower behind her left ear kissed her true said I must be this bird I don't know if I can live not see you again my love. She gets one tear in her eye told me to be careful, she smiled and said she will remember me that she had a memory, she kissed me and I leave thankfully she still loved me.

"One month later."

She moved away, fare away from me I do not know where. Her father's hand didn't allow this relationship between us two young hearted people. What she thinks? What she feels? I do not know. My heart break I'm in love pain my little sweet heart left without a talk.

Without a note I did not know, nothing where did you go, are you alright if I just knew. Did her heart break like mine her father a good man she said once to me but he no good for me. Because I'm just a young hearted man to young for this love, this two years love story of sweet love is over?

She disappears like into the night I couldn't see black like the night I lived so in one year.

My breaking aching heart healed at last. It took some time to stand up again. Oh! Love is not a game to survive it's a tricky way sometimes. But here I am strong like before. On morning when I woke up, I felt so good I thought something was wrong I did not feel any aching in my dear heart, instead I saw the sun rise stronger than before behind my curtains never forget this august when I healed at last. But I know my love for her is carved in my heart this is the end? Of my first love story?

Her name I still remain in my memory every day of my life and I miss her. I used to write poems words of love on the lonely night's to my missed love with only one wish, to find you, again in the crowds. will my wish come through with time maybe I will know.

(My love)

My love

you are on your own

fare away from me, the love inside of me to you

hold me though all these days

without you

my love

until the day I find you again

it's people everywhere

but no one there like you

my love

someday you will be found

in the crowds of people

I find you, again.

love will live one more time

I know you and me

is meant to be

'someday'

Early morning

Wednesday morning coming up today. These early days of todays. My old wristwatch 06:00 o' clock. I'm laying twisted tired in the light blue sheets in my big bed there I always sleep and find my rest and peace. But I must up, eat food to strengthen my soul. So, I get myself up to this young morning get myself ready for the day.

While I'm eating all my thoughts in my mind wandering to the memories of you my love

Memories of our sweet talk and when I kissed you on your cheek and nose.

That now rather a long time ago but it still closes to my heart the dearest part of me I miss our lovely talk we had these memories from back in time every breakfast day in my young life.

Now it's long time ago as I said I know. But in my mind, they always remain the same.

Year today is in the later 19th century. I lived my days in different ways, as this year went by ... All the people I met in my young life, everything inside of me like the love to you held me from this life pain inside of me oh! These days will I ever find them again. In someone else I do not know. How could I replace you, but a man must live needs more than a memory sometimes?

Nothing was like in the later 19th century that's there the memories was made with timeless dates. We all made timeless memories in my mind. me with you, my love.

Love is so hard to find someone say that special someone that get into your mind and heart and stay there. My lifetime filled with love as long as the memories stay in my mind it's a good morning to the day when the sun wait to rise into the sky once again.

This time I start to eat breakfast with you in my thoughts my love one more day one more time. Once again you remain to my mind as always it always stands the same, happy memories of these lovely lost days.

back from my memories I think she was the one, that name is carved in my heart and now carved in a stone? and I had one year's grief when I lost this love.

all I have left now is this memories of you, my love. they heal me so I keep them safe pick them up every breakfast day, with this felling I'm happy with what I got, myself and the memory of you. my love. These memories are in my heart they always remain in my heart our love always stay the same.

all my question inside, will I ever find someone like you again. I keep looking into the crowds after you. will I find something like this once again.

... the year went by these days without you I learned to survive it was no other options. but I still miss you. I miss our talk, I missed to hold you close, now you are gone and I still do not know where your father hides his girl of mine. I still have a hope we meet again to talk. will my wish come true time will tell If I find you again. maybe someday. I am longing for that day.

Every early morning, I wake up see the sun rise behind my curtains. I still hope we meet someday. That's my wish every day your name is carved in my heart always. I eat breakfast and hope you where here right by my side, wish to hear your beautiful voice, see your nice smile that smile you always giving me. Your father is a cruel man to me when he sent you away from me to keep the distance keep you away from me. It hurted my heart but I think someday will come and that someday we meet again. I hope our love finds the way we are a little bit elder now. maybe your feelings have change over time, that thought scares me. How about you are you still thinking about me, if we meet I see it in your eyes, your act. Is your love still there for me or is it lost, gone forever. do you remember me, maybe you miss me too exactly like I miss you. Oh! these days they come and days go but my love for you is there its whisper in my heart say I still love you, and that little whisper makes me to be patient with the thought to soon someday find you. You will see my face again. that's my hope. That day will make me understand if it be us together again, this little whisper is my hope I follow, make me look after you day by day until I find you, hope for this day it will give me peace then I will know if you still loving me. I have my hope that my name is carved in your heart too. And you still looking out for me too

In this crowds of people, you find me just like me finding you.

When our hearts still whisper 'l love you'

Soon, Some day?

I hope it is true that every day lead me closer to you.

All these days in my life, day by day they all passing by, and I lived my days as good as I could oh! these days so slow they went by. I missed the love we use to have, all these talk, all these words between a woman and a man

I miss these sunny days with blue sky above, these days. and to walk with you together hand in hand, again.

Everyone need someone I think its true and I'm sure I do not want to step into an early grave, to sleep. I'm to young for that the hope I have inside is this hope to see you again it saves me from the cold hole I'm sometimes almost fall into.

It's a hard life sometimes but I'm still looking out for you my love, looking out for your footsteps if I find them, I will follow them. Find you that is my hope Oh! Someday.

This hopes it keeps me alive these lonesome days.

All these questions inside my mind, my questions about you, us. are you still mine in your heart? where did you go? do you miss me? will I find you will our love be once again? and with an always thought where your father hid you?

I must find out.

So, hard life can be, I know now life without you. A woman and a man you could be my closest friend that stand beside me every day.

these thoughts and feelings are my blues in my life, it crosses my mind every day.

me, a lonely man this summertime I walk my way, try to find my way through. Hope the sky be blue with the sun shining above will I find what I'm looking for my love, you.

When autumn begins and summer passed away will you be there? Standing by my side every day? Even in the winter land. When the years passes by you stay by my side. Still holding my hand? Oh! What a summer if I find you this summer.

My love flower.

I'm all alone a lonely man now. Since your father didn't allow our relationship between two young hearted people. So, you left and move away. He sent you fare away from me oh! What a cruel man. I need our talk, your smile. Some of the last time we met I told you I don't want a marriage between us oh! Such young hearted man I was those days it hurted your heart so foolish I didn't understand.

A heart can break it not made of steel, I was so young and green. I wish I could ask of forgiveness to you, say sorry to you, my foolish words forgive please. I wounded your heart it was just a young hearted talk of me. because 'you are' the love of my heart.

I made some friends I met along the way. Some of them just for some days. That's my life for me I travel around looking for you, my love. I worked as an author of writing poems I wrote at nights. I didn't get so much money but I made it through the days I get money for food and room for the night.

The sunset comes, again. It's one more eve to live through. It is soon time to rest and dream for me, when it is a sunset there when the sun slowly sinking in the sky, my eyes see this beauty. so I let this beautiful night come, I let it fill me with recovery and dreams into my mind, this diving sun is the silent power of this night so, I hope it be some rest for me, so, let this sunset and night rule and give me good dreams and the rest I need for this night.

always every day when the sun sinking in the sky, I use to take a smoke and think about you, my love.

Nature is so beautiful so I have only one wish, to have company with you, my love.

There I stood and looked at the sunset, dreaming of better days I know they will come, one day I see you pretty face once more, so is my thoughts my love.

...after this deep sleep time for these early hours, it's time for the morning sun to rise again behind my curtain as so many times before, a new day arrives. I lay in my bed with the head on my pillow. I try to sleep a little bit more just a few minutes more, get some rest but I must up. I know to get some inspiration to write at night a little bit more I need some dollars. I will get it I'm sure because my days was rich because

I met some people that was interesting to know

We talked and laugh a lot together, some of the names I will remember a lifetime oh! Those beautiful days with my friends. I took some pieces with me when I leave.

As short I lived in the town.by town. They made some marks in my heart like love always do. I keep them close there in my chest. These little pieces of day and nights with some friends I met in my traveling days. When I look out after you, my love.

"One more night"

Tonight, it is a starlight's shine and a waxing moon is up in the sky. yesterday it was a new moon. Today it grows bigger and moon different light night by night so night by night it slowly will grow so, soon it's a full moon again. In this village they talk of the moon use to tell stories for the people, and children .said when it's a full moon they should pray a pray about some wish and with the white magic of the full moon it let the wish come true. Oh! All these stories, some people are very good storytellers in this village.

And I have some lines too, but to write. So, I put them down now some beautiful lines I collected from the day. Maybe something for you, my love. Maybe you read the news paper recognize my name, I hope so. I live and I'm longing for you, my love. My heart would break one more time if you left me for real when I still looking for you, my love., maybe you love someone else but me these days?

For every hour that passing by I'm afraid you meet someone else. I travel around ask everyone of your name I must find you, the clock don't stop times runs out day by day?

People like the poems I wrote in the newspaper. Lucky me. This way I get good food and room I needed for my days. The day started to go faster than before I wrote a lot with my pen these nights, time passed by quick and my friend for the day they give me good advice in life. And I told them about my journey about my life and I said I looking out for you my love.

These people were friends for life.

Then one day a friend said a new woman lives on the hill, working in the kitchen. Go there I think maybe if you are lucky its her. My heart raised in my chest couldn't breathe when I heard it, is it the same as my love. Her?

It took me some time to cool down, hands was shaking heart was raising. What's her name, is it the name carved in my heart?

Let it be her I said high again and again. All these years passing by and now, soon I standing at her door. Again. Heart raised in my chest to hear this news. Is it my girl I wonder awhile?

I'm eating up this meal to strengthen my soul. For this meeting, after that I walking slowly up the hill, I was a little bit nervous, and I had a long bit to go.

Up there I see it was a house, it was brown and had a little café' on the right side of the house. It was not so many people there they were just at closing time, I saw, when I reach the café' it was an elder woman inside. I walked there to her; I didn't see anyone else. When I reach her, I said my name and ask of a young girl, woman, working there? In the café'?

she looked at me, said she was in the basement, just wait I get her. The woman gets after her.

when the woman's come up I see it wasn't her. I be a 'little' disappointed. The woman was not her, damn.

I talked with her was she and the elder woman the only one working at the café? I asked, yes, the only one is us, she said. And her husband. I said I'm looking for my love and I told her my story in a shorter way. She understands and wish me good luck with that. And she said she was sorry to tell me nothing that could help me, so, then I leave the sweet café'.

I walked down the hill, with my head down I thinking feeling with a hope for better days but that day that someday is not today. Sad, I walked away. I met one of my dear friends when I was walking slowly along the way down the hill after I was leaving the little café'. My friend she asks me about the woman, did I find her there on the hill? But she needs no answers when she saw me hang my head and she saw a tear in my eyes rolling down my chin. She put a friendly soft hand on my shoulders, quietly we walked together side by side down the hill. Soon one more sunset to meet, alone and lonely one one more night. Maybe I write something tonight about sad love in my write, but with a hope of light it was so I felt. There at sunset when I take a smoke I write it all down and get some dollars for my room and food. My lifeline is you, my love. You save me from an early grave. You are the sun shine in my life and I hope to still find you, because I still love you. So, I longing for that someday.

I know that day will come so, I must carry on. On my own. Because I know someday I will walk with you again if I just find you.my hope is you take my hand so, we take us through everything. When we are together, we will be strong and we can carry on and on. Even if the road is dark now and you not here with me yet, I will hold you close in light in dark, I know because 'you' are always the love of my heart.

'When a man has a girl in his mind nothing can stop him' A friend I found this time said to me these words. We laugh a little to this truth in these words. A good woman we can live for that the happiness in life for a man. We both knew, these days we both men, we talked.

The power of a woman and a man nothing is like that. A strong man can cry, cry, cry. Cry of love. That's the power of love that's what love do. To give and to take that makes love circulate.

This nights with friends I had the luck to know them. Oh! what I will miss them when I'm to soon leave again, soon I must go.

...two days later, it falls a little rain from the grey sky, I leaved the village in the early morning and I know I left something behind, it is someone remembering my name in this village. Someone that talk good about my name people like that is good to find, maybe we meet again some other time. These wonderful days and nights a company with friends there in the village memories that will stay deep in my heart. Its riches my heart so I didn't feel so lonely with this love in my heart. When I went away again one more time to look after the girl of my heart. With way to go? I asked myself, I do not know, I go north and hope it's a good way to go. My compass is my heart, I trust myself I find you that's my hope you cross my way, that someday.

"My love I still see you like my love flower"

And me I'm a flower too I'm a flower. I'm one among
the others, no one more worthy than that other, we all
worthy, we all love flowers. Me a rose or a bluebell, you
a marigold or peony. Let us bloom together this
summer?! We be colourful with a good scent. Let us be
this lovely flowers of summertime. I have a hope to find
you this summer. So, that in mind I leave this village.
With that hope I have that strength until I find you.

So, I went away from the village by wagon and horse, it
was two beautiful brown horses, maybe five years age,
good age. so, I sat down in the wagon and the journey
begins. So, nice to sit there.

I was alone in the wagon so; I picked up a piece of paper
and wrote some lines. Maybe it gives me some dollars to
write. Must be something good to read. I wrote some
line about life, and was later thinking something about
my own life, my lesson in life. Something I learned in
life along my way was: that a naked skin, give thicker skin
with time, it was so sensitive to experience life. And
when life is hard, then you need a soft heart, and
whatever you going through you must filter it through

31

your heart/ that's my way to solve problems in life. I learned these days it's the better way.

It was a long trip to go, but it was nice. I seeing beautiful nature, to looking at it made me cool down. So relaxing. We stopped at a house where there was an old man that wishes step in the wagon. Old man with a hat. He was going to the doctor a little bit away, he said to me. We talked a little. And when we stopped again, I wished him well. When he went away

I was still not at the end of these wagon trip so I went away again in the wagon. Soon I should know, love of my heart was in front of us. But yet I did not know.

So, soon we was at he end of this wagon trip for me, and the new beginning of my first love story, but still, I didn't see it.

Still a little more to go.

Fifteen minutes later, the wagon stopped. There was a young woman in front. She had a big hat on so, I didn't see her face at once. The wagon stopped and she stepped inside. She sat down beside me. And then I saw something that made my heart raise, her nose, her sheek it was like yesterdays some year ago when I kissed her. Oh! My, my, my god it was her. I took her hand and I scared her, first. Then she saw me when I lifted up my hat. She said my name, and then. I kissed her.

She took my hand and hold them, we talked we laugh and cry of happiness. I told her that I had lived lonely on my own, that life had been hard sometimes. And I said I need a tender heart, and I asked her will she be that friend to me. I said I do not want to walk alone this road I'm on. When life is light when life is dark it would not be lonely to me if you my love hold my hand, this days we be together laugh , cry take us through every day. With love written in our hearts let us start today my love.

And now we are husband and wife, at last.

We now a woman and a man. Yes, a woman and a man, from day one we were the one. Listen to our story, as many years passing by, world roll around and we still stand as one. Heart pounding in the chest, all secrets we hide and our story together deep inside, the story of our life. Married now, after many days Oh! This life, this the story and history of a woman and a man

As husband and wife.

This time my love, do not let go of my hand.

My love flower.

"Soul"

The light of a morning

not everyone knows

how it really feels

to really 'see' the early light morning.

maybe life changes through life

one day if you not already know

you will see the glory

of a rainy, sunny cloudy morning

and feel it in your heart

'I live... One more day'

this day got a soul

what a beautiful morning

now for us, again

my love flower.

The year passing by like time always do. This time time went fast away like time do when its better days. Me today a man and a husband married with the love of my heart. At last, I'm happy. Every day I start my breakfast with a smoke and looking at the sunrise together with you, my love. Share this moment of nature. These days I start to smile again, it's because of you I have you in my life again. It was long time ago we could talk like these. And now I can kiss you on your nose again. A romantic feeling exactly likes in the lost days.

Oh! That happy day when I found you again after so many years. I remember it like yesterday but it is not fare away just about some months ago. I was there in the wagon leaving the village I had lived in for two months in my traveling days when I was looking after you my love, and then I sat there in the wagon, I saw a woman in front I didn't see it at once, she had a hat on, it was you my love I found you my love flower. So, this summer we bloomed together side by side just like my wish I made under the night of the full moon.

'I gave you, my hand. And you hold it now, my ring on your finger, the proof you are mine and I'm yours. Those happy days started that day. The day I found you again just about some months ago. It's a beautiful memory inside of me. Oh! That kiss between us two in the wagon I remember it just like yesterday.'

As I tell you is was some month ago, when I found you and my life started again. This beautiful day Oh! What a day. That day you stepped into the wagon and sit down beside me, you my love I didn't see it was you at once you had a hat on but then I saw, your cheek your nose I still remember after all these years. And I took your hand, first I scared you, then you saw me there under my hat and then we kissed there in the wagon and now we are husband and wife. These days before, a longer time ago when we were younger before your father sent you away from me and you went another way. I regret my words my actions, I talked without my head and heart when my young heart spoke those old days, I foolish said to you that I would never get married so, I hurted you with these young hearted words oh! What a fool I was these old days. What a punishment your father did to me, to us. He sent you away from me, all those years after, so lonely, sad, you didn't leave any note not a word, you couldn't. I didn't know were you were going. All these years I'm thinking about you, all the grief after you. What a pain inside of me. Such a sad memories the day you leaved and I didn't know were you go. Today these days today it better days after I found you and it changed my life to the better, it's about some months ago now. The clock is now 22:15 and it's a Sunday. It's a sunset so beautiful looking at this nature every day, like a painting Infront of my eyes. Now for us my love. What a good night soon I look at your cheek, your nose. There in the night light. It take my breath away to see you there and when you wish me a good night every night oh! What a happiness to see you smile like the old days every day and night now.

I do my best I try, do what it takes to make you happy. I use to tell you when day passing by day by day if it wasn't for you my love my days would just be wasted days. Because you are the love of my heart. Your smile telling me everything ok, it means everything to me my happiness is you.

I now become a man that grows bigger, stronger for every day, but sometimes I cry, cry, cry like a little child into your arms, I have a sensitive soul but that is not a weakness it's a strength you telling me. You like every side of me you say. My wish is to show you all of me let you see if so just a glimpse so you understand the real me and my hope is you love the real me. My Questions inside: if you were me what you telling me if your days was dark and I was your light talk to me tell me would you dare to speak with me and show me a piece of your heart to me. Your answers you give is to do that that is strength you telling me and that must be in a relationship between a woman and a man as husband and wife.

Our days went fast away in a fun way, happy way. It's like the colour of the nature grow stronger this is summertime green, brown, white, yellow, blue... all these colours for us. Since I found you my seances grow bigger, stronger as summer roll on. Summer went fast this summer, I remember I was happy every day and you were my sun. I used to say to you that you were the sunshine in your eyes even when the weather is cloudy outside. We talked a lot we made some timeless memories of the summer days it was you and me and the sunshine Like a dance we lived the days and soon the summer past and autumn begin. But I kept you warm, soon the winter arrived, cooler days we lived so we almost didn't know the weather outside we were happy and day went fast these days

Then one day we wake up from our happy days. You get a telegram a written message from your dear mother. She wrote that your father died in his sleep. That day colour of darkness I saw in your eyes. I have never seen you so sad. All days with your father they all passed away they never come again. Now everything just memories. Now it's like you not a child anymore you growing up fast these days oh! What you cried and you said it only exist one father in life and now he lay in his grave. Such a sad day. I do my best to comfort you we take us through we used to talk a lot about everything but time was hard for us now so, hard to speak so I hold your hand. Helped you through all pain, grief. To see you sad it makes my heart break again and again. I am standing by your side day and night until you someday stand stronger, remember me when you now dive into the darkness of grief. Don't forget about me. I tell you if we two for the road we are stronger, I hold the light for you just put your trust in me my love. I help you through I got all my love for you.

for some life is a long trip they live and tell every day of their life and for some life ends in a kick, so they get out of this life all to quick whatever times give to each of us remember the time we spend together in this lifetime and life itself 'is' a gift.

Your father had died at age of 'all to young'. He died in his sleep. Your mother and he they met each other in young age exactly like us, about 16 ages. They had a happy marriage and raised one daughter, you. Your father loved you much and because of that he didn't like me in my younger days, he thought I was to young to take your hand, and yes I was, then. But I loved you since the day I met you, and our secret love he one day finds out about, and then he sent you away from me. That was a heartbreak for me I didn't know where you were going. I felt it was cruel of your father to do so, but it was his choice to protect you from a to young love. All these years without you it was hard times and it took some time to stand up again, and it was one year grief for me after you leave.

Before I found you my lonesome heart it was missing you since you left, I was all alone so now I was lonely all on my own so, I just missing you all of the time, everyday inside my mind you were. There inside my mind and then one day I was ready to go after you. I had collected money through the year for this trip to find you. I travelled from village to village and ask of you it was a lonesome work but in some village I made some friends some for life. I wrote poems in the newspaper so I get extra good food and room for the night for my work.

Your father hid you well, I often wonder where you were, did you remember me? And miss me? Last time I met you longer time ago before you went away, you said to me that you have a heart and a memory, and that you only loved me. And would never forget anything about me. And I hope that still is so in your heart. All your love for me.

Maybe you meet someone else than me that thought scares me I missed you every day some nights I cried, cried, cried on my pillow oh! Lonesome me, but deep inside I had this hope to find you ,I lived for this hope, I lived for this day, because I still loved you. With that thought in my mind I often fall asleep at night. And I hope to get some rest for my soul in these lonesome nights.

These days I was looking out for you my love and when the morning sun rise again in the horizon one more day to live this way looking out for you, write, eat and sleep. It's like a wild cold wind blow hard in my life these days without you. I have to be careful where I put my foot today and beware where my steps lead me. My steps blure behind me so I can't find my way back, again. Must walk forward. The wild wind blow like an untamed orchestra in my life, I almost don't remember what I did or where I was yesterday only thing that's matters is where I am today. My shelter from a hard world, was you, my love. So all what matters to me is to find you., again.

I started the day with take a smoke and see this beautiful morning grow stronger. As the clock tick tock and day slowly goes forward. Soon it's time to eat some good food take me through the day exactly like yesterday. But with new hope every day that thought to find you everyday leads me forward and closer to you and make my love grow stronger as everyday passes by. I put it all down in my write words born by the day different word day by day it makes my day, its take me through this lonesome life. Now I will try to meet this morning, one more day in front of me, will I see you or get some information about you time will tell, now I must live this day, with this cigarillo I put the end of this smoke this morning, and start this thus day morning.

Strong after sleep I rose again

Your dear mother come to visit us. She come by wagon and horse, it was a long trip for her, but it was happy days for you and her to see each other again after long time. She wanted to see you again because her husband, your father and my father -in-law was missing now. Oh! I was so glad to see you, my love. Smile again you was so happy to see and meet your mother again. She was staying in our house for two months; she didn't want to be lonely now when her husband just died. It was good days in this situation when you comforted each other looking after each other, in that way it was happy days.

Together we stronger and we will carry on, just to hold on to each other that make us strong.

The funeral went by, tears and cry and sweet memories we all shared this cloudy summer day.

Your father got a stone. Now.

He lay in his grave.

Let his soul rest in peace, we pray. We remember his grace. Our different sadness, for you my love you miss your father, your mother misses her husband and for me I lost my dear father-in-law. Peace to his memories. We will remember the days but we must understand life is now. When we stand there beside your grave, we all wish peace to your soul, 'deepest peace. 'May the sweetest white angels sing and dance for you forever on your grave so you will rest and sleep with deepest peace into your grave these days. We may sometimes come to falter. In our steps, of loss and grief these days but we also carry lovely 'bright memories' of your lived days. Oh! These lovely memories give a rest of inner peace in our chest. Love was, love is. Oh! This happiness and grief. So now let it be. A rest over your grave today with both love, care and peace. A small blue flower we sat on your grave today which shows our memories of you is in brighter days you are in our memory and it will preserve throughout all the years of our life's. So now our dear friend, husband, father and father-in-law you think its now time to say this word goodbye?! But that will never be we will never speak this word from us because in the corridors of our hearts there you for ever wander so we keep you into our hearts there 'you' always be so, you stay forever with us, rest in peace, deepest peace. R.I.P.

Life was now hard but life went on. For your mother it was time to go home again, she was strong now. These two months had passed away fast. We called for a wagon and a horse and she leave with a hug and wishing well.

Now it was just us again in this house. Those beautiful days with you and me, happy us because we two for the road and we had grown stronger than before. Your father we talked about him every day until the grief let go more and more. My love never let go of my hand sadness in your eyes we take it away by love and time. I see you are sad: it makes me sad too, let us live through this pain and we must get our feet on steady ground with love we rose again. My love again and again...

maybe we must learn to love even the dark, after a while they say we can see in the dark. maybe that is true.

"a glimpse of heaven"

We started to live more and more every day. It's a good thing to talk to each other make some understanding about grief, its like a black hole we falling deep, but we rose again and again that was life for us this long year after your fathers death. We healed at last, so we could breathe again Oh! What a heavy year, but we was two for the road, you didn't let go of my hand we helped each other through. That what love does.

Happiness starts to find us again on this morning I saw a little smile in your eyes it made me smile too. I asked about your smile you said you had a beautiful dream you told me. A dream about your mother she was glad in the dream. So that's the reason why you smile this cloudy morning, this smile was born by the heart so we should share it. So, you called your dear mother and said you had this dream. She was glad you dreamed of her, she said. We laugh a little to this beautiful dream in the morning. You my love you had been so sad for your mother and then you saw her there in the dream smiling.it was like healing, like a beautiful painting inside your mind oh! what a smile a dream can make what a beautiful morning. she smiled so quietly there in the dream so you could see a glimpse of heaven.

Life more and more comes back to your eyes I was so happy to see you smile again. I feel you come back to life; the black grief was behind us now. It's now the green colour of summer time outside again in these warm days we keep us warm, we got each other that's happiness of us. Love is a power I pray we find the well of love everyday there inside of us. If we do we take us through.

Happy days start again, this early morning, with a glipht of life in your eyes I kept my trust to life. You were a little worried of all this grief, one cloud on our blue sky this new day was your feelings about your mother, you were so scared she will die too like your father. We talked a lot about that, you said you almost like an orphan now. And we talked maybe we must get our own little family.

With that plan we started to see our life in a different light. And here our new life started, family life. So we sat there in our garden with a tree with two little birds that sing us songs from morning to afternoon, what a beautiful day, we don't just let it pass away. Remember them they give us peace in our head with their songs of everyday. Listen to the bird's little song while our plan be real, more and more every day.

Soon we call 'grandmother' and tell our little plan and bring happiness back to life OH! This happier days in front of us. A family life for. Us.

Soon?!

We both feel this is a good idea, to build a family life now. It is like we have put down a good seed... into the good soil now. It will grow stronger day by day and be just fine. We share this new seed, this thought about a family life here in our little garden. So, with this seed in our thoughts we build us a whole garden.

☆

"If , our sky, loses its shining stars.

it is true, what people say.

stars can be re-created, be born new.

born, so our black sky, can get new shining stars.

That new stars be our light, in the dark night.

Shine for us again, in a beautiful night "

Universal truth

"A Normal Day. for us my love"

I s when We see the sunset go down in the horizon, I take my last smoke for this day. Today was filled with a lot of love. You and me my love we see this sun sinking, slowly, going down until it at last be dark..and it's time to sleep. Tomorrow is another day. All thoughts, feelings collected from this day we talk about before we put out the light.

I am so happy to have you by my side day and night. All this day's you and me, we experience the life as husband and wife.

And your grief fade...

I learned that open hearts can heal, so just don't close the heart...Let me in. Your grief after your father have fade a little more and more as time goes by. I use to remember you I'm always by your side, every day. So, we grow stronger you and me because we talked a lot together. That is our strength it takes us through. Our thought in our head we make some understanding when we put them out in the light. Have the guts to do that. That's a strength you say to me. You want to know what's going on inside of me, and I will tell you almost everything about me.

I trust you and you trust me. This marriage is happy for both of us, I'm happy as I can be, with a kiss I kiss you goodnight and you answers with that smile you always giving me. that's a good night from you to me. We get to sleep this late night and we rest our souls and minds until the morning light.

I know our love makes your grief fade more and more and I know your beautiful eyes will colour my day, day by day. Happy as I can be because you love me too. You say you got the eyes for me too.

"These days"

These days before I found you my love, before I started to see these better days with you and me, my love, and live my life again day by day. Before this I was 'on my own' I lived in a hard world. I suffered alone and the road was dark. Then and then when I needed it the memory of your word of love turned on the light so I see my way through. I was lonely with my thoughts, in the start, but met other people someone else that wanders this road I was on. I learned some songs, with them for those roads I'm walked along. With this songs I took myself through if it wasn't for you I would still walk all alone, without that someone that sing along. We like two birds on a wire now we sing together our songs. From morning to afternoon. Peace and love in our heads of this beautiful songs everyday we sing along, now happier songs these days as life go on...on and ...on.

My weakness is that I can't live without you. So, I can't stay strong on my own, that's the truth. Even when we are together hard times come hard times go, but it is easier to walk the road. Make ourselves through, it is better as two, I promise you. It is nice when someone stand beside me, when that one is you.

and I accept that weakness of being two, and the gift of loving you. It makes happiness come through for both of us, when we have each other in this marriage of us

"You and me (this is my life, today)"

happiness is to share these days and nights with you
every day, day by day. Today it's a new dawn, we had a
good night with a good sleep and in real life we both
dream about to get a family life. That is our talk today.
A little baby in your arms, and grandmother there beside
you. A little cloud in our blue sky these days you say you
are so sad, because of your father, his dead and lay in his
grave. He would be a good grandfather. You say, you
miss him so much but grief after him fades away bit by
bit by time and love. But we always remember his grace.
And it would be so fun to have him around, you say. He
was a good man he protected the family. Back in time he
didn't allow our young hearted relationship. So, he sent
you away from me and I didn't know where you were
going. He hid you well my love. But I found you at last,
we were now a little bit elder and more mature. And
your father accepted me these new days because of that.
And, yes, your father was a good man these new days. I
miss him too. It's a grief for us all he died all too young.

Now your mother knows about our new plan, to get our
own little family. She was so happy about this beautiful

news so, she cried out loud, of happiness. She said it was the best thing she ever heard in these lonesome days.

Me and you, my love we used to sit in our garden and while the birds sang, we used to plan this new life. talking about our feelings about family life. It was so nice there in the garden to talk with you, my love, yes, it was so nice there in the garden to talk to you and see the nature, and the light of the sun there for us, every day.

We sat in a lovely silence and relaxed a while my wife and me, it felt like an experience and an adventure when we felt the sun on our skin and see all these butterflies with their beautiful and colourful wings. When these small sensitive butterflies went down, and landed softly on the flower petals. The petals were still wet from the rain that fell yesterday. Nature feels so much stronger in the summer times, than it does on the winter days," I said" to my wife. Summer times its butterflies, flies, dragonflies, bumblebees... I mentioned too.

On these warm summer days, life of all of the gardens growing plants, gives 'new life' into the depths of our hearts. Can you explain? These beautiful summer days with your own words? try to tell me what you feel in your heart. "I said" to my beautiful wife. When we sat there in our own little garden. "flowers 'talk' with its colours and scentses so, it inspires all of my senses so, I know I have a heart. This is a flowers grace and that hit me deep in my heart." "She said" to me softly and thoughtfully. Then after a while she gave me a soft warm kiss and asked me for some words 'for that?' And it grows a little smile on her lips... and it was my time to speak, she waited...patiently, but I was...speechless. by the warmth, of her kiss.

Summer is such a beautiful time, but we all know flowers are sensitive; they wither and die with time, like this little one in the corner of our house. I pointed with my finger to the corner of the house. Maybe a little more rain and the sun will rescue this flower's life. If you want you can go over there and put some water from a can, maybe you can help this little withering small flower to survive, "she said." My wife is a good gardener she knows with the power of good circumstances nature can grow, and she says the healing power from nature, not everyone knows? nature it's a power, we all can grow stronger from it, find deep peace in our souls, and get a protection from the tree's when the cold wind blow. We use to sit there in our garden, we spend a lot of time there, to talk or sometimes have some lovely silence. And after a while I rose, and went away too be this... hero. for this withering flower.

"A good morning"

A good morning again, how could it be something else when you are here by my side. I smoke my morning cigarette. My little habit is to make fun smoke rings in the air and relax, and I used to talk about everything from within my mind, with you, my love. And I use to listen well in your talk to me in every way. I still see the grief in your eyes sometimes. Sometimes you speak from your mind and sometimes from your heart. Oh, what an interesting talk. You and me. I know you are the one that stays, if my whole world would fall apart, or if the world would just leave, I know to be with me is enough for you, just be with me, because you love me true. Our relationship is for real and I know you love me, true in your heart you stay with me.

So, you are my closest friend, and my wife my love flower. You colour my day everyday with your beautiful eyes.

Love went back in my life the day I found you again. What a luck. You are my love flower again. There is only one queen in hearts in a pack of cards, for me you are my queen in hearts I use to say to you, my love. And let us talk through this Wednesday afternoon like we love to do. Like we always do, maybe we will find out about family life a bit more.

While the birds sing their songs for us there. When I find the sun is in your eyes. again. There when you talk to me. About everything, there in our colourful green, brown, yellow, blue, white. Garden. Just for us, my love.

'A mother', you try the word, you tell it out loud. Taste it.

...feels good, you say. You tell me after your father's death you felt lonelier, like a half orphan. And You tell your mother you love her dear and you miss your father. Your mother and fathers' marriage are over now. She's a widow now. They got many years of marriage. It was a long and happy marriage. You loved them both.

Your father was the head in the family and your mother was the heart you talked. And you were their only daughter. You all love the life of what a family could bring. Your heart was your home. You had Family life in many years then your father died your mother lost her dear husband. All to young, your mother she was happy she had you and now...soon...she will be a 'grandmother.

That pick her up from the black hole of grief. She has something to look forward to. It strengthens her soul. She was longing for the future now. Our little family plan strengthens us all.

'My wedding finger'...

Time went by.. and my ring still fits me on my wedding finger, I use to say, a ring of gold. I do not want to take it off, I'm proud of it, it's the proof I'm yours and you are mine. A sign of mature love, and responsibility, a sign of I'm your man and you are my woman.

We walk through life together a piece of my heart I give to you, please take care of it. Rest of my life I give to you.

We both know give and take make love circulate inside of us, remember me. If the world be black like the night, I hold the light for you. I love you, yesterdays, now and tomorrow's that's my promise as long as you love me, I keep the ring of love on my wedding finger, my ring still fits me after all these years.it still burns on my finger.

"October"

The flowers bloom of this summer is over for now but it come back next year just wait and see this beautiful flower they come back every year, so, with these thoughts we now leaving the season of green grass, yellow, red, blue flowers, brown and green trees, rain and the beautiful warm sunny days. And now autumn begins and we know it will soon pass fast away and winter land soon arrives with colder days, snow and ice.

Together through the season we live day by day. Days went fast away for us.

This colder October day today is the day I will remember the day I felt like I was a loser, a loser, of faith in love. When you my love said you must be on your own, questions inside my mind wake, don't you love me anymore? Are your feelings gone? You wish to live on your own so, you left me. You moved away to your mother to find answers. And me...I cried, cried, cried.

Oh! So lonely I felt there on my own our garden is soon filled with snow and ice again.

Our little garden there we used to sit and plan our future of family life.

Now I start to wonder a lot again ...must I find a new path on my own? without you my love, after you leave me, the path I walk feels much darker and much colder this rainy October Saturday morning. I take one last walk on these old paths of yesterdays. paths that were our paths. These days today they all just passed away? They just bittersweet memories inside my mind. In my head I wish I was home, with you my love and never needed to start a lonesome walk on my own these autumns day and I feel every step I take is in the wrong direction when all I wish is to walk back home to your heart, my love. But in my aching bleeding heart that home is gone now? Exactly like you? We are at this crossroad? you went another direction in your heart? Oh, these crossroads they hurt my loyal heart. You leave me forever? Tell me the answer. Are you gone forever? if, my heart will break for sure. you said you need time to take a break thinking about your life and me. heal from your pain and sorrow inside of you.

These days apart hope you think of me, miss me and longing back to me, my love. My love who am I without you, nothing, nothing at all. I pray it will be better days for me, us. That you come back to me with open arms and never leave. The day or night don't know what is worse. It feels like the days is a waste of time. Night only a pleasure when I can get my sleep, my only rest. I can't make myself smile anymore. You left me lonely with feelings I can't handle on my own?! You not return? Oh! So lonely I felt these days without you. and the shadows of darkness that is life for me this day today. Only you can change my mind of thinking if you would come back, my way of thinking would completely change, because if you got love I believe in 'you', in us. Again.

I wish you back by my side again and that you would take a serious step back into my life again and stay until my dying day. This is a big dream but some dreams never come through? My dream only exists when I daydream or sleep and dream of you?! and there in my dream you are fully alive and we live a good life. But when I wake up you disappear only me is left in this world when I wake up, I'm so alone. Because like a bubble bursting 'you gone'. this is how I feel today.

Time went on. When you had live with your mother for three month now, and finally we met and talked. I wonder if we could find love twice between us again. Give us a second chance, and you surprised me with a yes'. You said you had think it over hard again and again, and you said you missed me a lot this months and had cried in your loneliness. "So, can I come home?," you asked carefully and I answered with a smile, this was our start to our second chance.

And these time the luck find us. Once more we growing stronger together than before. I got back my faith to love. You take my hand once again and you said you won't let me go alone anymore. And we seal this promise with a kiss, now it was us again my love. We two for the road again my love. Once again you were mine. And once again the winter land arrived. We were ready it was you and me now. We keep each other warm when the cold north wind blow. That's us you and me happy as we could be. We maybe soon be this family we dreamed about.

As people see we are together again, we decided to give it one more chance. We both know we love each other, for real.

We know better to take care of each other these days.

we learned if we take care of ourself and listen on ourself it can take us far. So, it is up to us and listen up and follow 'our path' ('path of heart'. I believe 'the path of heart' always leads to the right destination, it leads us home to safe ground 'these thoughts we must keep in mind. In reality we know it can be hard to live a life in peace and harmony time after time when hearts can get crushed all the time in reality but we know if we stay strong, we will see love repeat itself, endlessly.it makes us strong, when we feel weak. There is no end what love can do help us through so we know to not give up keep our fight between right or wrong find our answers in our mind and heart. So, we get us self through one more time. and if we listen up and remember if we got love, both of us, we can both say" I believe in you."

When I was on my own, it was a hard world. I suffered alone when the road was dark for these three months without you, but your words of love turned on my light in my heart again I started to see a future for us again. So, I see my way again I'm not as lonely as I thought someone else wander this road, I'm on, it's you. We learn some songs for those roads we walk along. With these songs we take us through. If it wasn't for you, I would walk all alone without that someone that sing along with me. peace in our heads of this beautiful songs everyday we play along.as life goes on on and on.now. together with you again, my love. Love songs from the road lived by us. About life ups and downs I wrote songs for us. As we sing along.

I found out those days my weakness is that I can't live without you. So, I can't stay strong on my own, that's the truth even when we are together hard times hard comes hard times goes but it is easier to walk the road make ourselves through its better as two, I promise you, it be nice when someone stands beside me, for me it's you.

I accept the weakness of being two and the gift of loving you.it makes happiness come true for both me and you. When we have each other. The marriage of us what a beautiful strength and weakness.

"Baby cry"

Happy baby cry all over. Family life started when this little baby was born on a rainy Wednesday morning. I remember I remember it just like yesterday. These beautiful memories that will stay deep in my heart forever. The birth of the children it was a big moment to us all. A new family member peeking out in the light on 15 of august. At 07:34 then a baby cry started in the air the cry filled the room. A little baby girl... and yes, another baby girl came out in the light at 07:43. Now we were a little family, bigger than we planed from the beginning. I was now a father, husband and son-in-law.

I was proud of the babies they both had 10 toes and 10 fingers. I was so happy. Oh! This moment it will change me to the better. I know my life as a father will changes me forever year after year to see my little family, my girls growing up. My wife smiled the birth of three hours was over and she was a little tired but very happy. I kissed her on her chin we both was a little tired I went after coffee and a sandwich to strengthen me. Oh! These Wednesday what a happy day for all of us this Wednesday started the days of our family life. This little baby girl's grandmothers dream now she find peace and happy days every day. The future is lighter than before. She gave the babies their names she said my little babies. And she said she will love them until her dying day. Said she will pray for our new family members so their life be filled with love and grace. Oh! Little grandmother her smile told me more than words can tell. And me, I was so proud. So, that night I fell asleep with a soft big smile on.

Grandmother is in the kitchen, baking and cooking meals for a whole company, us. she love it she say and her daughter can rest a while after this heavy week she said. We had so much to talk about, the two little babies changed everything. The light had return in grandmother's eyes she loved life again... after her husband died and she be a widow and left her so lonely so the babies now become her life. The family tree was growing and everyone of us was glad for it.its so exiting life now. Everything was so new for us but we loved it. Grand mother said she feel younger again when she sees the babies, they both so sweet. Two little baby girls what a surprise it's like a present on Christmas eve. And it all bring new life for us my wife and me talked a lot together before sleep. She said she will not forget me because of the children she said I had a place in her heart and that will be, we are a family and a husband and a wife too. And I answered with that smile and said I loved her and we had a good night, now we go to sleep, for eight hours, at least. I thought. But... you know how it is...with little babies.

To wash diapers all of the time that's what we do, it's life for us now and what a luck we are a team in cleaning diapers the babies eat and poop all of the time.

Outside the windows it fall a little snowflakes we are a bit in October month and soon the winter lay behind our door. We have a fireplace in the living room wife and the babies use to sit there it make so beautiful memories to see them. I used to look into the fire place and feel it is like a fairy tale. Everything changes for the better day by day. Life grows stronger and my best habit is to smoke my last cigarette for the day and see the children fall asleep a happy moment every day I say goodnight to them, they use to wake in the night then me or my wife go and check it out little babies they talk a lot their own little language we try to understand, sometimes we do. They have their own vocabulary between them two.

Now we have our little family as day rolling by day by day, to love is what life's about.

So, for today ...have a good night. let us end the day and this story with this poem I write for the night:

Child

My funny little child

so, young at heart

live this life

as good as you can

put a little pray every day

pay thanks for everything

you have

you are blessed believe in that

if you need some faith

you will pray for that

careful what you wish

you may get it just like that

get to know the power of

yourself

inside your soul

make your day then rest in

the bed

dream time, dream a little dream

take a little nap

the night is there for you

relax my child

and remember I love you

until the end

of time

The end of part one

DIAMOND

♥

Part Two

The years is in the later 19th century. So, let me tell you the beautiful truth of today, that is, that me and my lovely wife and our two little babies are my life today, My whole world. Every day when the sun rises, I'm in my thoughts thinking that I am a lucky one. And yes, I am. It enriches my life, colour my days to see them, when my wife's happy, beautiful eyes meet mine every day. I see more love in her eyes these days after the babies been born Her beautiful green eyes, they for real colour my days day by day, that's the truth. Of today.

The small children with their special needs of love and care, food, sleep... We share this work between us every day. We work well together I use to say, and my wife says she has the eyes for me she tells me I look like a real dad, and she is happy to be my companion, she says it with a smile, and I tell her I love her.

We notice the babies grow fast and time runs away. With time we be competent in handling the children we say to each other that's true. And Your mother use to 'educate' us in baby care. The babies are twins and look exactly like two cherries. We use to talk with them and the babies talking back a lot with their own little noises. We try to find out what they really say to us and each other. They 'talk', poop, sleep. smile... All of the time.

We are so happy with our own new little family. It wasn't so long ago we sat there in our own little garden and made all this planes for us. Now that plan has come to reality. The babies arrived and maybe they are just two 'little' girls, but they are so precious for us in our world. We are now a much bigger family than what we had planned, it was two baby girls peeking out not just one, one like our plan was from the start. Three hours it took the birth. all went well. The day they were born I became a dad for the first time in my life. It was a special strong feeling to see them with my wife. Both new born babies were laying naked with their head on my wife's chest, so peacefully, and holy This moment and memory are for me. I will save it in eternity.

Me, a proud dad, with shoe size 44, a grown-up man, with a gold ring on the wedding finger, with a happy heart and a good wife I love to talk with. I got everything I need, a family here for me, a real home. That's why I always have a big smile on, that's me those days. It feels like I got a good life. But I know it's a big responsibility to build and live a family life. I will learn more and more along this way. We are two for this road: me and my wife, with our little baby girls, our children. If it needs, I would die for them. I used to say to my nice wife, and she used to say she would do everything so I never get in that situation. And she gives me that smile. I just love.

'I'm happy. I have a faithful husband and a companion. I have done the birth of two babies. two little baby girls, I'm proud of it. And my dear mother maybe she's a widow now but her strength these days is the babies. Together we strong'. My wife looks into my eyes and says these words to me. She is so happy for this situation. She almost gets one tear in her eye but not of sadness but happiness, real happiness. She looked me in my eyes for a while and she started to grow a smile and said that the plan we did in our garden for this family it's the best thing that has ever happened these days. And she thanked me for my love with a soft, warm kiss. And me. I said I loved her, that made her smile, that beautiful smile she often gives to me. That happy smile, I could die for.

Yes, I die right on the spot if I have to, I would give my life for you. And the children. I do everything for you, my love. You know it's true. Because without you my love I'm nothing, nothing at all. Love is and will always be the biggest thing to me.and as I said I love you, my love, and the children, my family is everything to me. Yes, I would die right on the spot for them and you.

It's like a friend in the village said to me 'a good woman a man can live for' and I feel these words are so true, from this dear friend in the village there I lived in when I was looking out after you, my love. These words...so, true.

Sometimes I use to miss these friends in this villages I travelled to, this village by village. And Some of them I will remember a lifetime. I miss these long nights with my friends. May I ever see them again. I would like to tell them I find my girl. Not just any girl, but, The girl of my heart. I told them much about you and they gave good advice for my life. I miss them. When I was in need of these good advice, when I felt lonely, when my days was dark, they led me back into the light.

Now its morning light shining from the window. It's time to end this smoke, this Sunday morning.

And today we say good morning again to the little babies or is it the other way they the babies wake me, often there is them wake me and my wife. They often up before the seven o'clock. And me, when I wake up every morning, I'm just longing to see them. My little babies.

My wife and me use to have a schedule for the day, sometimes it includes grandmother too. A schedule about the babies, dishes, food, cleaning and other stuff. When grandmother is with us. Like she often is some of the weekends, she just loves to cook food. So, she often takes that part of work. We see if it is a happy cook, it gives a nice happy good food we think. If she wants to cook. We were all pleased. There is gunpowder in the 'old lady 'we use to say, a little humorous. Both in her way of do work and the way she cooks. We were both satisfied with her time and work. We love her very much.

"Now is the time to move"

For your mother it is soon time to move from that old big house now when her husband, my father-in-law and my wife's father had died and buried. This house there your mother, you. (My wife) and the father of the house had lived in younger days, here in this house there me and my now wife had our meetings these younger days of our life. That little lamp with its soft light in the window in her room, I remember that little light I used to look after. Her message she was home and it was ok to climb that tree. And visit her. Oh! Such a wonderful memories, the father of this house we remembering him he didn't allow our young hearted love, when he one days find out about it that we had a love affair for almost two years. This time I used to take a ride with my white horse to this house, throw a little stone on the window if the lamp was on. So, she heard the noise of me. Then she opened the window and helped me inside, as so many times before. our romantic room. We called it. We smile to all these memories today; they are very sweet. And innocent. And we keep these memories in our hearts. In the depths of our hearts. Oh! such memories. And now I'm married with my first love, this girl. I hope it be a forever love story for us. I use to look on my wedding ring and I feel so proud. Me I have a sensitive soul my woman like it so, it's a luck for me.

So, now soon your mother must move from this big old house, with all these memories inside, it was too big, to her now when her husband is dead, and it is also to fare away from us. Now when the babies born, your mother want to live closer to us. now, she can't visit us often. Now we see her only on some of the weekends.

We loved to have her in our house, so, she is always welcome. Our home is her home too, we said to her. She was so glad, now these days. She loved the children. She loved to cook and talk; she talked a lot. So, when she leaves and go back home it been so quit after her. But soon she's back at our house once again. It's always a pleasure to see her. She as I said talk 'a lot.' Maybe it because she is a Gemini, in astrology sign. I use to have an interesting for astrology. I use to read book about that. The Gemini sign is all about communication, they love to communicate. And that's my mother-in-law.

I read a lot, your mother she talks a lot and I read a lot. It's so exiting I must tell you. I read and I write, often at nights. So, I often see the sun set in the horizon. Like a beautiful painting in front of my eyes. I use to share these moments together with my dear wife. I take a last smoke for the day and see the sun go down for this day. now is the night.

A new dawn.

A new dawn is here for us, one more day, one more time. The nature is so beautiful.as always it uses to take my breath away.to see the sun rise and turn on the day light for us. It's a new day here for us. A new dawn What will happen today. We will come to see with time. The clock is 07:10 o'clock. And it's a Saturday Its early, we are up. Time to eat. It's nice to eat together with my family. Before all this I was on my own. The days was all about to survive. It was hard to be alone on my own. So, these days it's nice to have a family. Before we eat, we use to pray together and say thanks for everything we got and thanks for the food on our table with a little ... amen...in the end of the pray. Yes, we are so thankfully for everything we got. Never thought life could be this good. We blessed.

My wife and me we talked a lot when we eat, I love to listen to her interesting talk, she is very open to me sometimes, she says it must be this way. She wants us to dare to talk about everything in our life's. She sometimes is open like a book to me and yes, I just love to read this book. This is my best book in life. I use to tell her. A book with no ending always a new page every day. Something to find out in every chapter. Our life together I hope it will be a thick book. My days with you, my love. We write some history. I use to softly wonder why, why, why you must argue all of the time I wonder sometimes inside my mind, but whatever you say I love you every day because you are in my heart and when I thinking about it all, those argue make me to a wise man in my heart it makes me think. So, I love to listen to your interesting talk. And me, I often remember my wife, about the important to 'live, love and laugh' to do a smile every day that like strong medicine, I say. We can never get to much of it. So, take your time to laugh, love and be yourself. Then you have the chance to be loved for who you really are by yourself or/and by someone else, that is true happiness in life, I use to say to my wife, and she agree with her sweet smile to me.

So, this day what do you want to fill this day with today my love, I asked Curiously. She answered thoughtfully after a while and said love, a lot of love and a lot of you my dear husband she smiled and the babies. I want to fill the day with love. Let us do that I said and kissed her. Oh! I think I heard the babies waking up. A baby cries.

The day start for real now.do your morning toilet my love, I take care of the children I said, she smiled said thanks and went away to get herself ready for the day. this Saturday morning.

Next time I saw her She had put a nice green and white dress on, and she had fixed her hair. She really looking nice my wife. She used to change her hair sometimes. She was good in this. Sometimes she had her hair free, sometimes in a hair tail, knot. Or a hair braid. I have a beautiful wife. In every way. And she's mine, I thankfully thought. And we danced through this Saturday. Happy as we were. We easily filled this day with a lot of love.

And next day, and next...

"Change of season, to autumn"

Time went fast away and Season change, it's now time for autumn, these cooler days. We lived through these days one by one. Monday to Sunday and Monday again. Again, and again...

Until the day stopped

My queen of heart, get the cold. your nose was red and you had the flu.my Poor little woman. It is never nice to have the flu. Just to hope it doesn't pass over to me or the little children. because who will take care of all of us then.

So, these days while you were sick, I'm taking care of both children and you. Lucky me your dear mother supported us during these heavy days.

I was happy for that.

You my love you were sick for over a week. And then one day you felt stronger. Me, my time as a nurse was over. you felt strong now and felt good health again. Me, and the children and your mother none of us get this flu thankfully. And now you kissed me for the first time in over a week. Oh! What I have missed it.

"The cold winter days, arrived"

The cold winter days arrived. Soon it was the first Christmas with our little babies. But they are too small to know its Christmas. But we buy presents for your mother, because she worth it she had helped us so much these years. And you loved your mother so, much. You had made a warm cap to her so; she would not freeze. You had worked with this cap in the eves. now it was finish and it be a perfect Christmas present to your mother. And you buy chocolates for her too. You know she loved chocolates. It was always welcome.

We had a fireplace in our living room. It was cosy, I must say. Warmth of the fireplace this cold winter days. We were all in this living room. Me, you my love, the two children and of course. Your mother. We all felt well. This Christmas day.

Your mother lived now in her new house, it was not long way to her house, we almost were like neighbours now. And that was good it had been tricky way to handle she lived so far away before. then it was long road to go between us. Now it was almost like next door. This way we see each other more often. Almost every day.

We celebrate Christmas together. It was nice. We exchange Christmas presents, eat a dinner. Your mother and you done in our house. It was a turkey with potatoes and a lot of nice food. The Christmas was nice, couldn't be better if you ask me, the only man in the house. And your mother she just 'loves' the chocolates.

"My Work"

I use to think and write in my work. My thoughts about life, and the weekends, is that...some days feel short, especially the weekends. Friday to Sunday is there for your rest and entertainment so take a deep breath and relax soon these weekend days passed by I hope these days is good because we all can find the ordinary days 'Monday to Friday' heavy like 'hell'...sometimes. somethings never change

And that is why we will have a great time when the weekend days after this 'heavy work' come again.

Oh! This work, work, working days to work can be fun but exhausting. Everyone needs a rest. That's why we be 'free 'on the weekends, to rest our body, minds, and soul. But me. I love ordinary days. I love to write

I work as an author, write poems, stories and other stuff I have done that now for a long time now. When I was out on the road and looking for you, my love. I used to write a lot with my pen, people like my write, I used to write for the local newspaper and other papers and magazines. It gave me food and room for my days. And after I find you my love I kept this work, it gives me some money and I do work with something I really love to do. Write. Its creative, interesting and fun. I hope people will keep and like my writes. Lucky me. They still do these days.

My wife she does not work for now, but I do not know in the future. She comes from a rich family. She has been born with money in her pockets I use to say to her. So, for now, she is home in our house and take care of the children. she thinks this is an important work, that's her work at this moment, she uses to says so.

We are happy both of us with what we do, and we respect each other And we have time for our family and each other that is important, you tell me often. This that we see each other and have time to talk, and listen. Is something that is close to heart both for me and you, dear husband. And we must to have time for grandmother too. Time for life, live a good life. Take care of ourselves. That our work too.

So, because of this we now these days today we live a good life. Our love feels so strong and true between me and you. And I hope and wish it will never change but I know someday it can change, so, is life, it can change all of the time. If it does, I believe we take us through like our love have always do?! Our love is strong, I know, and it makes me hanging on. So, I have all my hope in you, us, my love. If we would come to a crossroad, again. Like we did a long time ago now. I still remember that day when you and me drifted apart you wanted to be on your own a while. It's the day when I woke up from my, our, dream, dream of a family life, that day it felt like a lost dream was left in my hands that day, bittersweet Like sand through my fingers I couldn't keep it?! It was lost I thought, when you leave. all this love we had and our sweet dreams we shared about to have our own family was gone?! I thought. My hope then was that you my love would come my way again. (Like you later did) If, then I would come alive again it was my hope these days. So, I wish you will keep to hold my hand and don't let go. Because I want you to know I follow you wherever you go. So, please don't let go of my hand, my love. Don't say goodbye because I'm not that strong how would I survive? When to lose you is the worst thing in life. As you said that day, when you come back' you do not let me to walk alone anymore'. So, with these words I think we take us through Everything we meet in life. As long as you stay by my side, I feel alright and believe in love and life. My life depends on you, my love. I trust you again, like I did before. Let me do that, don't give me any reasons to doubt you, I trust myself I think you are a good 'woman' that's my faith today so, now it depends on you, my love. As you said: 'you will not let go of my hand anymore. Let that be true, my love.

We use to talk like these my woman and me.

Because no one knows what the future holds.

So, we must take care of everything we got. If we don't take care of it, it all will Wither like a flower, fade and die.

That's why I call you my love flower. My love.

"Monday a winter day"

I like art and I have a favourite painting hanging on my wall. I use to study this painting and look on it. It is a middle age woman, painted in oil, by an artist, sadly unknown. I love this painting it is good art. And she smiles "she talk so wisely there on the wall, with her mysteriously smile" I always thinking she don't need to talk, she need no words, still, she always be heard with her mysteriously smile she smile herself deep down into my heart every time I look at it... And I read books too, yes, I do, a lot of books. I have always loved art and to read and write maybe I like to read because of I write a lot or the other way. As I tell you I have always liked to read, books, papers, magazines poems. Yes, everything. So, that is interesting for me. Like a little habit I like to use my ABC. And my mother-in-law she loves to talk. The happier she is, the more she talks, I use to notice. So, these days she talks 'a lot'. And I am happy for that it always so fun to listen to her, she's a wise lady my mother-in -law. And I have the luck to know her. We have a good relationship between us. Me and her. That's good isn't it.

My wife uses to talk too. when she talks with her mother they often talk about children, love and care, family stuff. Her mother like 'educate' her. And then some other time my wife talks to me about all stuff the learned about family life and family stuff. It was that way I find out that my mother-in-law is a wise lady. How would we survive without her.

All her advice, love and personality. All what is her. She is a widow, she says it's a little bit lonely on her own, like a new world to discover. But it's sad that her husband never gets to know our little baby girls. It would have been so fun for all of us. She uses to pray for her dead husband, were ever he be in heaven or hell or something between he knows shall know in his heart he be loved by us still. Even if he's 'dead' and not are with us in person down on this earth. We remember his grace, and his strength, Amen.

"Thursday eve"

Today I sit down in my favourite furniture. I have a little lamp on with the right light and what I do, is I read a book. I use to sit like this a while almost every day. To read, to reflect. Over the words, the story I read. I like this time I have on my own. So, nice and calm to sit here, read, writing, thinking, about everything. The book, it's a luck to find right book to dive into.

My wife uses to tell me I look so innocent and sweet when I sit there on my own with my head deep down in a book. She says it look like I'm in another world and She knows how much I love books and this moment when I take my time to read. She knows almost everything about me, these days. I love her much. She let me sit there on my own she does not want to disturb me at all. So, I sit here, today it's been about three hours of my time I'm concentrate to this read. Very interesting read. I will continue tomorrow. Something to look forward to. So, I put away the book on the little table. And I take a smoke, a cigarillo a little pause before I go to sleep.

My wife brush her teeth's and she put off her clothes. I see her body silhouette in the soft light. Today she has a little sweet night dress on, it's a little cold in the room. It's still winter land outside. She doesn't want to freeze so I hold her warm in my arms. We talk our night talk and then I turn off the light.

"A month later"

My wife talk sometimes she feels I'm yearning, for love. And she tells me that. That I have a sensitive soul. She like that sensitive side of me she says. I know it, she has said it before.

I am a lucky guy. Me the sensitive man. Only She understands me I use to tell her. That's true. Who can understand me more than you, my love.

I always love our talk. You and me. My love.

We have been married for some years now, I use to have the gold ring still on my wedding finger. I do not want to take it off. It fits me. On my left ring finger. Still. After these years.

We still man and wife.

And I still love you so. My love

Now, its breakfast now and a Friday, its family time. We sit around the kitchen table. Eat and talk. The little children are with us. Every day like this. Before I find you, my love. I was on my own and it was hard times so, this moments with us all I really love. I know how it is to be alone all on my own. To have two children is sometimes not easy. They need care and love. As us too my love. I think we are a lovely family. So, fun to be together like this. You understand the children so well. We learn to know them day by day. And they growing fast. We take care of us selves and each other. It's important. When we finish the meal I the man in this house do the dishes and you my love you take care of the children its Friday, time to take a bath. The children love to bath. They use to laugh; smile the sign they are happy. That make us happy too. Now we are going to have a great Friday.me and my wife use to drink a glass of red wine on the eve when the children get to sleep it's a beautiful moment so, relaxing for both of us. But at this moment its some work to do before the eve. So let us live this day. As good as we can. And I'm longing for the eve this time just for us, my love.

Oh! Yesterday...what a great day. I said softly to my wife. When I lay in our big bed with my head on the soft pillow, with my wife beside me. its Saturday morning. Me and my wife had a glass of wine yesterday and we had a dance, yes, we danced in our living room. Just me and her. We use to dance like these a dance only me and her. So, nice and relaxing to dance this Friday eve.the children slept; and it was a good night.

"Monday, again."

Work, work, work I must work I feel. I feel I have the flow now. So, I write it down. On paper. A story. There from inside my head. This is good I say high to myself. I got the flow. it took me a long time some hours to write it all down. All day. And I felt again, this is good. And yes, the magazine loved it. So, I get some dollars for my work. I'm proud I said to my wife that they like my write. When we were drinking a cup of tea' in the kitchen. Maybe I shall buy you that red dress for some of the money my love?! She answered with a smile. And this day passed and I know I will sleep good to night. Before that I said good night to my little girls, I saw them fall asleep and dream away to this world of fairy tales. And I kissed my wife good night too. Tired as I was, knowing its some nice hours sleep in front of me, I fall asleep after five minutes. And I slept the whole night trough.

Good morning, I say to myself when I meet myself in the mirror the next morning, think it's Time to take a shave. I have had beard for a while and I used to have beard oil in it.but now I take it of it is my wife wishes. If she wishes this I must obey. So, these is what I do. Oh, I almost not recognize myself. I thought when I'm finish my shave, I look younger version of myself. I wonder if my wife recognizes me, maybe she thinks it a foreigner in the house. I shout for my wife, and she comes running, I think I scared her, but then she sees my new me. She put her right hand on my chin feel it say it so soft. She congratulates me to my new me. I smiled and kiss her. She says it feel a little different now, and she say she's pleased, very pleased. She said I was like a new man.now. she says she must get used of it. But she's pleased. She also says she love me both with or without a beard, but she says that the beard was tickling when I kissed her before, and she give me a blink' with her one eye. And she went ahead the kitchen to making a cup of tea'. And it's her turn to shout after me. 'Tea' time darling.' she shouts after a while. and I come running.

It's so nice drinking a cup of tea' in the young morning with my wife, the children take a little nap now, so we feel 'free' now. She smiles and look me right in my eyes with Her green mature eyes. Oh! I just love them. I want to look into them rest of our life's. my wife is a cancer astrology sign. And me ?.. I am an Aquarius. And she uses to say she love my eyes; she loves my true-blue eyes. And she smiles. And we have a good morning.

It's so quietly in the house, it still early, children still sleep, soon they wake up. But not for a while ?! so, after the cup of tea' with my wife. I take my time to sit down and write. My wife does her morning toilet, a little extra this day today. It's time for her to wash her long hair.it smell so nice after wash, like a scent of apple. It always does. I like that scent. her favourite shampoo.

I really love her, this woman. How could I face reality without her. She is my strength in my life, she's intelligent, fun, and caring for the family, she's a cancer a family person. And me an Aquarius, an air sign with a lot of thoughts and a writer. The day grow stronger, go slowly forward, soon I guess the children wake up. Soon. But I have still time to write... this morning.

My wife passes me by, she sees I'm writing she ask me, or suggest me, can't you write something about the children. and yes. I can, after a while after thinking I wrote this:

("Bond/ with your heads on the heart, like a pillow, you rest your minds, in this beautiful moment, calmly you sleep, what a beautiful sight, two new born Childs, on the chest of a mother, at this moment, love become the bond between the children, and the mother.")

I write this when I thinking of the birth of my children, it was a strong moment to see them the new born babies on the chest of my wife. The day I for the first time in my life become a dad.

My wife read it and loved it. She like my sensitive side.

and when I was on the go with my writings, I wrote one
more, about chess and life in the old days. Like this it
goes...

"Chess, is an old noble game
for the intellectual ones to play
the one with a brain.
dressed in black... Or white
you move the pieces around.
and in the foreground
a less? Worthy pawn than the rook and the knight?...
a game on life and death
play the king out like in the old days.
the mission is to save
the king and his queen, so move your moves
knock out the other side
just like...In the old days

Now, the children awake, I can get them, I go for them,
my wife said, and running away. To take care of them.
And me I continued to write...some more lines.

"The visit"

The time is in, it's time to go and visit grandmother, she lives in her new house now, In the nearby, not far away. She had sold her old big old house and now she live in a smaller house. She lives there by herself. She says it's so quietly without her husband. Only noises are the birds. Nice colourful birds. She likes the bird because it isn't felt as lonely as it would without any noises at all. So, me, and my wife and the children we go to grandmother with wagon and horses. We see this house for the first time it is bigger than we thought. We say to each other. Nice house. When we reach the house grandmother open the door and wave with her hand like a little hello! So, lovely to see my mother so glad, my wife says. And we wave with our hands a hello! Back. We stop, stepped down from the wagon and gave a hug to grandmother. then we all stepped inside and... wow... what a house. Was the first thought, It's even more nice inside than outside. I say to her that she done a good affair, if the rest of the house feels and look like this. And grandmother smiled and said yes, it does. Oh! Mother I'm so happy for you, for us. That you have a house now and it close by. Now you can come and visit us more often my wife said and whenever you want, I said. And grandmother said that we are always welcome to her place too. And then we sit down, talk, and drinking coffee, she surprises us with a cake, she said she baked yesterday, and we celebrate this moment with the new house, the children and the good situation. The children slept in their little child carriage. They stayed calm all of the time. Mother talked and talked as she always does, after a while I went outside to take a smoke. While they had their Woman talk. When I stood there and take a smoke, I thought I am a lucky guy. After I had stood there a long time, I take a walk, a little walk to look around. It looked nice. It was water a little bit away, there we could put a boat and there were woods around, yes, a nice place. This will become one of the child's childhood places. I think it will be just... Lovely. And I went back into the house. When I was taking of my shoes in the hall, I heard they was laugh and they talked into the kitchen and I smiled a happy smile for myself. Before I went back in to the kitchen. to my family.

"Next morning"

At breakfast me and my wife talked. I thought exactly
the same as my wife, 'it is a nice house and a good
situation', all this, I said to her about the water and the
boat. And she smiled. New Future plans. We can sit in
our garden and give birth of new plans. She spoke. It
exists a future for all of us, I said. I'm so happy for this,
she said. And me, I agree.

Sun rise, a new day is born I must get something to do
with the day. I spoke. to myself in my thoughts. Today I
must work, had some papers to write. Earn some dollars.
Maybe I shall buy that red dress to my wife, little new
clothes. With a nice colour. And maybe a jacket to
myself. I thought. Before I start to write my ABC...

Work is done, completed I had the money safe in my
pocket and a big smile on and was down to the store. So,
the red dress from the store is now inside my wife's
closet. And a new jacket hanging in the hall.

"Some years later"

I f I look back in nearest time, the nearest years I can truly say we had a happy life. All of us. The children have grown up a little bit more. Your mother, my love. She is still alive and we guess she have a lot of years left of her life. She uses to say that she saves that 'last dance' to some other time than these days. When death of tango is the final dance, when it's time to bite that black rose and dance that passionate dance of life and death, I better have good dance feet so I can dance myself out of that last dance. Of tango on life and death. Everybody must dance 'dance of tango' someday. She says, and That's why. I don't like to dance; grandmother use to say to us. And we, can I say we still in love? I think I can. I have a heart and I see with my eyes you still happy when I'm around. It is almost more love now than before, love has grown. That's for sure.

We more mature, we, the children. and the evidence is your mother still talk and talk... 'a lot'...

As she uses to talk more and more as happier, she is, as I used to notice.

And that boat, yes, it is in the water now. for long time ago.

Life will go on, on and on...and on...that's life.

As long as we love. 'We' be alive.

And when we are all together, we be and feel like a real 'diamond', unbreakable.

We and our little family.

So, ...I open the window; it is summer time outside and I feel a soft wind sneaking in. I feel the warmth wind on my skin I got a family here inside. And I take care of everyone. As the warmth wind sneaking in when I walking back to the kitchen. Happy as I can be I'm thinking I have my own family.

...and our family grows stronger through every day, week, year that we go through...we live, we laugh, we cry we think and act in life we do this every day again and again. A mix of emotions all of the time that's life for us.

Oh! My dear little family you are my treasure and I am so happy I went after you my love, in those now old days, these younger days. When I'm finally find you there in the wagon, I remember that kiss between us two, my love.

Oh! What a happy day after Those old days when I was looking everywhere after you, I was alone all on my own.

I looked under every stone and 'finally' I found you, my love.

I knows I want to look into your green mature eyes every day of my life now. I know I will love you until the end of time. You and the children are my life. Like a diamond we shine every day in this life, and I will be true, give my heart to you every day and night I'm there for you. I love you my love flower.

The vision in my head says the future is said for me, it's you, for all the days, its true my heart is filled with f.o.r.e.v.e.r you, thank you. When I'm yearning for love you give it to me. My sensitive soul you handle it so well, because you understand me as only you do and you do it so well.

We are a family and a husband and wife. We write some history you and me, every day. Let us write something good today, something exiting tomorrow and something with love every day. Let us take care of the day appreciate the moments in life tomorrow there are memories in our hearts. memories can last a life time.so, because of that let us live well. Everyday.

And every time when I look your beautiful green eyes, I feel I come alive. And that little smile, that little one that grows on you, on both of us, when we look deep into each other's eyes we both live in these moments. And when the years pass by you are still by my side. It's a beautiful weakness and strength for you and me. Let us live through the day, just by to look into each other's eye's. And to see that little smile grow. That makes the day come alive. That's life between a husband and wife. You and I. the hair will with time, maybe, be grey but our eyes stay the same through the years.

I love your sweet green eyes as you do with my blue eyes too. And that little smile. Oh! What a great day to be born, every day.

Every day...

So, my dear wife I hope your days in life be kind, and I wish you joy and love in every step in your life. I stand by your side, if you are in need, I hold you close. In the corridors of my heart, you always have a place because I loved you from the first time, I saw you. And my life with you makes every day to a sweet memory. I'm a lucky guy to have the luck to have you by my side. So, what can I say but 'I love you'.

Now it is time for Thursdays eve sunset, the light fades more and more, it's get darker and darker the sun is slowly sinking looks like the sun is slowly diving down into the horizon line, my wife is yawning, this day was so exiting day. We lived every hour of the day. Now we are at the end of this day. The clock 'tick tock' so, here comes the beautiful darkness with its rest and recovery, at night we feel free to use the time to rest and sleep, or maybe a little cuddle too with heart and soul. What it be tonight we do not let you know because now we turn off the light. We say good night, to you now.

☆

And now, at last

one more write before the night fall

about, and for, all love artists

all over the world.

☆

(If)

if, love was a colour

it would be every colour in the palette

we mix them together

and make love with

every shade in it

ex: red and white together

it's pink

a romantic colour with youth in it

passion is deep red

maybe something for the adults

I think passionate love is like the colour

of red.

like the pulsing blood is red

it something pulsing inside

without it you would feel dead

use all the colours in the palette

to express ourself

so, create like the true artist

we are

without this colours life would be boring

every day of our life

we would feel dead

so, take the brush and

stroke a colourful lovely rainbow

Or peafowl of it.

if

if love would be a colour

it would be

every colour in the palette.

The end of part two

Diamond

Part three

The birth, of the two children for some years ago, it has change ourselves to the better for all of us, thoughtfully.

Me now a more and more, with time, a more mature dad. before this I was lonely, life I lived was hard when I was on my own but today, I'm not lonely. me and my family lives in a house out on the country side and the children's grandmother lives nearby she is a careful speaker and she use to speak a lot of Lovley words these days. it is so much going on inside this woman's head and she is happy to share it with us. She is a wise woman. And she uses to live an extra healthy way in her life now. She says it the one and only way now when the children exist in her life these days. She has not time for dying she say. now when the children make her so happy.

She's been a widow for some years now and she starting to get more used to this. Her husband is in great memory wherever he is, she used to say.

She really misses him some days. She says she still falters from loss and grief after him, some lonely nights

Myself I am still in love with my beautiful wife. And I will walk the line as long as she loves me. We are a good match for each other I learn to know as year after year goes by, I understand I am a happy man and we live a happy life together today. Time for us is day by day went by but there are no empty hours for any of us, we always got a lot to do. Especial when two children are with us.

I myself read and write for us so we get food and clothes. My interest is to write. It is like I always got a lot to write, and that is good, I often write at late nights. Maybe it is because of all the collected thoughts and experience from the rich day. I like to sit down and do my work. Different thoughts every day. I find them and write it down.

My wife uses to inspire me, with all her suggestions. She got a lot in her head this woman and she is mine I thinking, thoughtfully.

"Saturday morning"

Saturday morning coming up.it is time for some work, not writing, but time for some other necessary work. We need some wood for the fireplace in our livingroom.so I went outside and went to the woodshed; I cut some woods and picked them up in my arms. Placed the woods in a nice woodpile. I think this will do for a week. Later it is lovely to sit in front of the fireplace. It is the coziest place in our Livingroom when the light fades and the moon rises on the dark sky in the winters and the warm fire sparkling. I love to sit and see into the flames and talk with my wife. At this moment I feel life is good.

"On the eve"

My wife is a creative and handy person, she handles the summer garden well on the summers. and she use to knit too. She is good in this, so I use to say she could even knit with just one stick. She loves colours and she chose them well, she mixes them together in a fantastic way. When I sit down and do my writings she uses to sit on her own too, with a lamp beside her in her favourite furniture, a soft rocking chair. She knit fast. She knit sweaters to the children they are still small in size, so knit these sweaters go fast. These home-made sweaters it is interesting to follow when she works quietly in the eves with this work. She uses to hum by herself when she sits there in her rocking chair. Knitting and humming. Its nice to put on warmer clothes when the sun hours getting shorter and shorter and the temperature is sinking. The small children are in bed and they are sleeping so it it a quiet eve.

My wife, after sitting there for a long while, my wife got up and went into the kitchen. When she passes me, she asks me if I want a cup of black currant tea, with bread. I thought for myself it would be great so I answered her with a "yes please", and she went into the kitchen. And after a while she came back with a tea cup and a plate and put it beside me on the little table with the bread beside. I thanked her again and enjoyed my tea. After a while I rose myself. I was a little stiff after I had sat down for a long time.it was a pleasure after tea to take a smoke, a cigarillo, there on the porch. The temperature was lovely, cool, but not cold. it was a great day, both of us was creative today, and the clock 'tick tock' quietly, it was the only sound from the kitchen. After a long day. Its now time to recover in the night. With this day activities we both pleased so it had been a good day. It is now time to go to sleep. But I'm longing for tomorrow, one more day with you, my love. You and me and the little children, my little family.

"Next morning"

Last late night the cold north wind had been too strong so a tree breaks down and put itself in the way. It was time to put on the coat and warm hat when the morning light arrived. Because the tree was blocking the way.

It was heavy but with the power of a strong man this tree was soon of the way. Winter days like these do not happen so often. The tree I took it and cut it inside to our fireplace. It always so cosy sitting there in front of the fire, in the warm light.

My wife is a very caring person, she thinks so nice this wonderful woman.so I can't find the words of all I feel in my heart for her. I'm so grateful for her. She is my inspiration, my life. And she is the mother to my two sweet children. we have a life together. And it is a rich life to live when we are together as family.

"The winter this year was cold."

The north wind blow like it used to do on some winter days, days was short and the dark started to fall early. Inside the house it was a fireplace, with it warm light to sit in front and drink chocolate together with the company of thoughts of the loved ones. Always so exiting. I'm a rich man I use to think.

The cold winter is over now and warmer winds is here today. When I open the porch door a warmer wind sneaking in and I'm smiling for myself I'm looking forward, soon the first spring flower will catch my eyes and the beauty of summer will grow fast as it does in this next coming season. In the season of summer then we will see the power of the nature, it can change day by day I know. Soon time for summer again with green trees, green grass and a warmer sun, rain is also welcome for the seed we need both sun and rain for this land.

I stand on the porch take a smoke a half cigarillo. Thinking about this day. Time passes by while I stand there on the porch, thinking and wonder about life.

On the eve I have a favourite book on the shelf I use to read. I often sit with this book and read it again and again. Every time I read it; I see something new. I like this kind of book. Some writers are good at what they do. I'm a writer myself, maybe some readers like my book too. Books can be good for the head. A pleasure to read, learn something new, spending some time whit a good book is nice.

When the stars shine above into the sky, I use to take a smoke on this beautiful winter night and summertime I use to look at the late sunset and see the sun go down in the horizon before I turn off the light and get my rest and sleep through the night.

I really like nature. Sometimes when the weather is good, I use to go fishing at my mother-in-law. Her house is near a lake. That boat is my weekend pleasure, sometimes.

I have always liked the nature, its so peaceful and it makes me to a better person.

Through my life I have had luck or the head on when it comes to people. Some people are tricky people. I feel I have learned to notice troubled personality and keep myself on the other road, on the right road. Road of health to choose that way makes my life good. And that is you my lovely wife. You put me on the good way.

You talk to me; you dare to say the things I need to hear. So, I am a lucky guy. And you are a really wise woman. Just like your mother.

It is Sunday eve I'm tired, my wife too. Grandmother went home to her own house nearby after visiting us. It has been a joyful day with both laugh and cry, child cry. We try to raise our children right so they make themselves stay alive in this bigger world. They must help and take care of the house. Know the important of a home. Everyone needs a soft spot of their own and that often come to be home. They obey our wishes, learn day by day and they start to be good in this. They understand it more and more every day. Where to go but home. When you need to calm down. Sit in front of the fireplace or on the porch, the fireplace with fire sparkling. Is there any better place to be in the whole world, but home. We try to make them understand, if we not got a home, we have nothing. Where do you sleep? where do you keep your personal stuff? where do you breathe? where does your heart rest and live? when we need to pull the coat closer to our chest when you need a shelter somewhere, where to go? tell me? At home, where else.

"This summer"

The sun rise behind my curtains. It is a Monday morning coming up. It looks like it going to be a great day. It is quiet in the house, the only sound is the kitchen clock ticking, peacefully. I'm a little bit elder now not old but more mature and my young heart has growing up a bit more. My wife still sleep she look so sweet and the children sleep deep still.

It is so quiet and I like that at this moment. Sometimes when I wake up, I am in the middle of a dream. I feel it is nice to dream sometimes. I use to write about my night adventures. I do not want to wake my wife she looks like she's in another world at this time.

So, I rose after a recovering night. I have slept well and it is time to put my feet on the floor carpet. With time I came to be a morning person. I use to rise up like the morning sun I'm often in a good mood too. I enjoy life now. I got used to it, life is great. I step up, after fifteen steps and I am in our kitchen. I put on the water to make myself a cup of tea. In this young morning. I like the scent of tea. And I use to sit on the porch with a blanket around me and look at nature. And smoke a half cigarillo. And when I sip it up my regular cup of tea and I sit there in the light of the dawn then in my mind I'm thinking "what a beautiful dawn."

This is time on my own and a good start on the morning. When I have sat there a half hour my wife opens the door to the porch and sang a good morning then she stepped out and sat down in the chair beside me and she asked if I slept well as she often does. We sat quietly and looked at the sunrise. A really good morning. My wife does not smoke but she sometimes takes a glass of wine, just to relax on Fridays. After a while we rose and started time for breakfast.

After breakfast life started for real the small children woke up and needed their care and attention. Time to feed and handle them. We use to do this we try to learn every day to handle the children, it is not easy sometimes but them are well with themselves and we are a nice little family. We learn to know each other every day and it is a pleasure. I'm looking forward to it every day. To be with my family. But I also need my own time to sit and read on my own.

My wife uses to fix in the garden. She like flowers and colours, she is a handy person and she really know and understand to plant the flowers right. some flowers bloom in different times so she choses flowers so it blooms almost every day. She is good in this to mix the flowers.

Our little garden is a sacred and relaxing area. We love to sit there our little safe place. A perfect place to talk about life and thoughts. Sometimes it is good to sit on our own together as adults. The children are our sweet children but it is nice and I needed to talk with adult person sometimes. It makes me safer and it be more mature talk when I need some advice. We all do? Some days don't we.

Sometimes when me and my wife argue or are angry on each other, we remind both of us to act adults. We can't behave like a child, throw food on each other or scream at each other, I think you all know what I mean. I think we all have our own experience of that different kind of behaviour. If I am angry on my wife, really angry, I use to write on paper what I want to say and give this paper to her. she reads it when she feels it ok, think it over for a while and then writes back if she is angry too. Or it feels right speaks with me. It is a good way to us to communicate sometimes. It is a clever way to speak if and when we need. I think this way we have saved and rescued our nice relationship many times. And we still not yet killed each other. Act mature act that's better, much better way.

I cry sometimes. I am a sensitive person. I cry and let the tears roll down my chin. My wife loves it it makes her smile that little soft sweet smile I love. She's mine and she understands me. I'm a lucky man.

And to write is interesting. I'm glad people like my writings as I said I often write on the eve or late at night. I use to sit there with myself thinking, twist turning the thoughts, and write some line down on paper. This is my work. I like to write, today I will try to write something about the mind and the light. Hope you enjoy it. I was inspired by an old painting I saw on a wall when I was traveling from village to village. I call this write 'play with the light' So, listen up this is how it goes: 'What the night hides in these shadows of darkness?. In the dark we can heal, we can hide in this hideaway of darkness what is to be found in this dark? sometimes we will never come to know its to dark to come to show. We need both night and day, dark and light in our life. We can hide, we rest. In the dark. We show in the light. So, put the right thing on the right place otherwise you can be like a clown with a pie on your nose. So, put your hideaway safe switch off the light and with light, light up your day switch on the light when it feels alright and keep the switch safe keep it only for yourself. So, it come to show or not. What you do. Or don't want wrong/or right person to 'know'

I love art, it can inspire to write, art can talk..it is just to listen.

As a person I am calm, often in a good mood, a reader, a writer, and hopefully a nice father to two young girls and a sensitive husband, morning person and a cigarillo smoker. And I try to act well every day. I know it is important, and it is more mature. Choices we do, it can be good for everyone to think it over, we will try to raise our children this way. Raisin our children is not always easy and sometimes it is good to talk it over. So, both me and my wife teach the same to the young children. well, the clock never stops but I always try to have time for the important thing in life. What is important we can all ask ourselves sometimes. just to 'breathe' is important. Many things are important and we only have one life so we much all do our choices with what we do with our time. I hope my wife finds some time with me is important. Time together strengthens our relationships. Time tick tock so now it is time for tea with my wife and some crackers with cheese. Our afternoon tea we always have and our morning tea too. Time to sipping our tea now in porcelains cups and listen and have an interesting talk. Catch up some time with my beautiful wife, to have a cup here for you and me, when I sit here beside you the time always run away, I value this time, tea time, with you. My wife has her hair in a knot today she says it is nice to have this knot. It feels like she changes her hair. It feels like she can have short hair when she has this knot, and when she realises it will be long hair.

She also has her hair in a tail or bun or braid sometimes. Such an interesting quality time, time together is, even to sit quietly together make sense.

I'm looking forward to sitting down beside my wife and just spend some time, tea, crackers and you, my wife. a splendid mix.

The children are awake, they come stumbling on their bare feet through the hall and we hear their noises. I tell them to put om some socks so they won't freeze. My wife smiles her soft smile and we break up from our quality time together with just me and her. Now it's time for the children, to help them get dressed and eat and time for the pot. They can sit on the pot, self. I think they think its funny and exiting. Small children have other 'hobbies' than adults. We learn to know them. They have fun every day. Feelings change often for the children. they smile, cry, scream. A mix of emotions and we feel they are fully alive this way they are always so sweet, whatever they do we love them.

Time goes fast forward and we are now in the middle of the beautiful summer.it is weekend it is Saturday morning and we are early up time is about 08:00 am and the weather is fantastic. Me and my wife and the children went over to grandmother's house. Me and the two children will take the boat from the shore and go out fishing out on the lake. My wife stays with her mother in her house. Because they have a lot to talk about 'woman talk' I used to call it, they always have a lot to talk about.

I knew, inside the house, these two lovely woman's were now reading in the recipe book. While me and the children were outside in the fresh air, fishing and talking. It is a beautiful day. The sun is high up in a clear blue sky. I saw the children and they were happy. We all like to fish. We put the maggot on the hook. I helped the children and then we throw out the bait. The lake was like a calm mirror and it was a lot of fish in the lake. And the fish was hungry so after a short while the fish was on and on, on the bait. We will not be emptyhanded this morning I spoke. Later when we caught enough fish we went back to the house. We put the fish outside and went in for salt and knives... I show the children how to handle the fish. I said they must be careful with the knives and I show them how to cut of the head and the rest. We gave grandmother fish and saved some for ourself.

My lovely woman's had baked in the kitchen it looked very 'sweet' and very nice. It looked like a chocolate cake and of course we are allowed to take a bite. Me and the woman's had coffee and the children had milk. It was nice, and tasted like a dream. it was a great day and time went fast away like time does when it is fun. This was a very nice family day. After a while we must break up. I kissed my mother-in-law on her sheek and the children and wife gave her a hug. We thanked each other for the day and went away. We were going back home with wagon and horse. Grandmother looked after us when we went away. We all waved with our hands and grandmother waved back. And she looked after us until she could not see us anymore when we disappeared with the wagon behind the hills.

First then, she turned around and opened the door and went back inside with a happy smile.

Finish

"Dreams take them out to real life,

or let them stay safe, inside your heart.

whatever you do

have dreams

then you always got a beating heart "

"In the mirror" twelve years later...

When I see myself...

in the reflection in the mirror on the wall.

I see every wrinkle, and I wonder 'am I getting old?!'

the wrinkles all tell me about and reminds me of all the days I went through.

I think that all this happy time has been running by, just like 'a blink in the eye'.

it feels like my life has been running fast through. and like in a happy way I spent my days through.

all my good and bad days these days feels like a blink in the eye and I know they not come again, one more time... I know I not be any younger for every day and I learned I must live these days, day by day. because life is 'today', every day.

because forever is not existed in life everything that be born will die someday.

what can I say, some days, but forgive me for my bad days, bad days is the days when I sometimes forgotten about myself, these days just some days. Days when I didn't take care enough of myself...it happens everyone someday.

and if I could get my wrinkles and lines to tell me a story of my life, if I let them speak what will they tell me from inside, from my lived days. I think if I would do a colourful painting about it, it would be with a picture of a happy curve I would stroke a big vivid 'smile' on the cloth.

and it would be grief, and pain of passed days that not come again and a lot of joy and love too... I have mostly happy days in my life. but bad days too. I learned that's life for everyone.

and I find a lot of maturity, of all these feelings I found inside, through these days.

I live my life. and still find myself smiling these days with a little wrinkle now beside my eyes. I call it maturity what else? when I take a look into the mirror what I find is myself.

mirrors reflect this moment of truth. when I see into you, I see me, happy to see you. every day I meet this reflection of me. I live so I will love myself when I look into the mirror next day.

And today I feel... I still alive and live a happy life these days. So, I give myself a smile into the mirror...one more day... But I am learned life can be tears and pain and a lot of other feelings too, life can be like a mix of emotions it is like spices in a meal, we don't want to be without them.

Isn't it so?!

last writes

⊕

'Navigate'

If it sometimes
come to be some stormy waves?
on our sea.
we must understand
'no one can control the weather'
only thing we can do
is handle the sail
sometimes we must put down
the sail
let the storm pass
after that we can raise our sail
again
so,
we must all learn to read the weather...
...and learn to
navigate too.
take a closer look
on the compass rose
it will help and tell the way
so, we must all learn to navigate
in different stages
of life
if we do
our family ship will
sail safely through.

(Diamond the ship)

My ship, my family, my crew, my life.
by this time, you all heard I have experienced a lot of
HUGE waves, high and low.

I have sailed on the seven seas, on the darkest nights
...and with the sun high up on my sky.

I have my ship's flag high...where ever I go.

I'm the captain on this ship with my own crew.

I tell you of my adventures, I think
you already know (some,) maybe you have
a ship on your own? every ship has its own crew,
and their own flag.

together we sail the seven seas.

I do not leave my ship, I think you know the story
of the true captain and his ship how, it goes.
"With true love in his heart a captain stands

at the wheel,
even if his ship, his heart...go down...all the way
to the ground."

We all know, we can't control the weather only thing
we can do, is to put up or down our sail and let the
storm pass, after that we can raise our sail...
and SAIL...again.

We sail forward, when the sun dives into the
horizon line...at the moon shine...and when the sun
rises again we ready...to meet one more day again
My family, my crew, together we take us through...
traveling over the seven seas.
experience the adventures of a world of our own.
together as a crew on this ship
we raise our flag.
the flag of "DIAMOND"
this is our flag.
high up
in the sky, this flag, our sign
now I feel...up there...this flag
there it will...forever flutter

The end